Sick Day

by **David McPhail**

Holiday House / New York

Copyright © 2012 by David McPhail
All Rights Reserved
HOLIDAY HOUSE is registered in the U.S. Patent and Trademark Office.
Printed and Bound in March 2012 at Tien Wah Press,
Johor Bahru, Johor, Malaysia.
The text typeface is Report School.
The artwork was created with ink and watercolor.
www.holidayhouse.com
First Edition
1 3 5 7 9 10 8 6 4 2

Library of Congress Cataloging-in-Publication Data
McPhail, David, 1940-
Sick day / by David McPhail. — 1st ed.
p. cm. — (I like to read)
Summary: When Boy is sick, his friends Dog and Bird
try to help him feel better.
ISBN 978-0-8234-2424-5 (hardcover)
[1. Sick—Fiction. 2. Dogs—Fiction. 3. Birds—Fiction.] I. Title.
PZ7.M478818Sh 2012
[E]—dc23
2011026153

Boy is in bed.
Dog sits.

Boy is sick.

He is cold.

Dog helps him get warm.

Mom helps him get warm.

Mom gives him soup.

Dog gives him a bone.

"Chew it," says Dog.
"But don't eat it."

"I have soup," says Boy.

"Keep the bone."

Bird comes.

"Boy is sick," says Dog.

Bird goes away.

He comes back with pizza.
"This will help you get well,"
says Bird.

"That is good," says Dog.

"But Boy has soup.

Soup will help him get well."

Boy has a nap.

Dog has the bone.

Bird has the pizza.

The next day Boy is fine.

He and Dog go out.

They see Bird.

"I am sick," says Bird.

"I ate too much pizza."

Boy and Dog sit with Bird.

Then Bird is fine.

But Dog is sick.

"The bone is gone," says Boy.

"I ate it," says Dog.

Boy and Bird sit with Dog.

Then they nap.

Dog jumps up.

"I am fine," he says.

Boy, Bird, and Dog are all fine.

It is time to play!

I Like to Read® Books
You will like all of them!

Visit holidayhouse.com to learn more about I Like to Read® Books.